NEW Y JOGRAPHY

A Fun Run Through Our State!

by
Carole Marsh

This activity book has material which correlates with the New York State Learning Standards for Social Studies. At every opportunity, we have tried to relate information to the History and Social Science, English, Science, Math, Civics, Economics, and Computer Technology LSSS directives. For additional information, go to our websites: **www.thenewyorkexperience.com** or **www.gallopade.com**.

Gallopade is proud to be a member of these educational organizations and associations:

The New York Experience Series

The New York Experience! Paperback Book

My First Pocket Guide to New York!

The Big New York Reproducible Activity Book

The New York Coloring Book!

My First Book About New York!

New York Jeopardy: Answers and Questions About Our State

New York "Jography!": A Fun Run Through Our State

The New York Experience! Sticker Pack

The New York Experience! Poster/Map

Discover New York CD-ROM

New York "GEO" Bingo Game

New York "HISTO" Bingo Game

Table of Contents

What is "Jography"?

Dear Parent, Teacher, Librarian, and other readers,

Haven't you ever heard a kid pronounce geography joooography—as in, "I have lots of 'jography' homework but I left my jooography book at school and we have a jooography test tomorrow!"

From the reports that we read, that kid may very well flunk that "jography" test. What a shame that such a vital, interesting, essential subject has been so short-changed. Why is this? Perhaps we thought geography was boring when we were in school. Maybe it seems to change too much. Just when we figure out where a country is, it changes its name, capital, and government! Or are we not willing or able to visualize the world as what it is— just a big neighborhood?

Whatever the reason, I hope my series of "Jography" books helps make geography more exciting and interesting. Never before has geography been a more important study for students. Through political and environmental concerns, we have found just how important it is for us to know where our neighbors are and what they are up to. And the world is growing economically smaller. A child's future career may take them further than around the block! They are almost bound to be involved with other countries and their language, cultures, and money.

But the best place to start is out our own back door! Perhaps geography does seem boring or useless until someone gives us season passes to our favorite team's games. Then all we have to do is figure out how to get there. Now that's motivation!

So, the approach this book takes is to consider geography from the kid's point of view—what they may be interested in, plus to communicate that geography is history, economics, politics, art, science, communication, etc.

Thank you for helping kids get hooked on "jography"!

Carole Marsh

Some Down-To-Earth Reasons to Know Your "Jography"

I'm goin' to the big race!

Recent studies show most people know very little about the places in the world in which they live.

Sometimes it's as important to know where somewhere isn't, as much as where it is (unless you like catching the right plane to the wrong destination or vice versa!).

If you don't want to learn too much about a place, at least hit the high spots so you won't sound dumb or insult someone. But even more importantly, go ahead and learn a lot about a place you're interested in. After all, in today's truly global economy, there's just no telling where in the world you'll find yourself calling on the phone, putting money in the bank, or traveling to by plane, boat, or rickshaw!

What's "Jography"? It's a way to explore a place that's just a little more realistic and a little more fun. Most people don't even know much about the geography of their state until someone gives them free tickets to the big game—now all they have to do is figure out how to get there! And I'll bet if they announced there was money growing on trees in Kalamazoo, you'd have no trouble finding out exactly where it is!

So, put on your jogging shoes, lace 'em up tight and let's go on an armchair journey. Like any true traveler and serious geographer—of course you can use a map! Look in an encyclopedia, atlas, or ask your parent or teacher until you find a map that you like and that makes sense to you. Then see if you find the answers to some of the following questions. I'll bet you discover them and a whole lot more!

Happy "Jographing"! And for fun—keep score!

Which way do I go?

New York "Jography" Word Search

Before you get started, jog your memory! You've heard of most of the geography-related words below. Find them in this word search. Hint: You'll only find them by latitude and longitude! Score one point for each word discovered.

```
C H A R T X L I D E G R E E O C E A N
O P O L E Z R H E Q U A T O R X B M N
N D G L A C I E R X U I S L A N D N B
T E M O U N T A I N R U Y L A K E M O
I S A R C T I C P L C I V O L M R J A
N E R I V E R X J O V W I N D U R P C
E R T D E L T A Z N E G L O B E M R S
N T I Z O N E L M G R V O L C A N O X
T R O P I C S X C I B E A R T H M A P
G L V J S B V M K T I D E W A T E R L
V V A P S L P P L U C L W Q P M F C A
D U B L A T I T U D E P I E D M O N T
P T N A L L X I N E W Z M R P O I U E
O G R I D E V K J H R E G I O N S P A
X P E N I N S U L A M N B C X H G E U
```

Word Bank

CHART   DEGREE   OCEAN   POLE   LATITUDE   EQUATOR   GLACIER   ISLAND
MOUNTAIN   LAKE   ARCTIC   WIND   DELTA   GLOBE   ZONE   VOLCANO
TROPICS   EARTH   CONTINENT   DESERT   RIVER   LONGITUDE   TIDEWATER
PIEDMONT   PLAIN   PENINSULA   GRID   PLATEAU   REGIONS   MAP

MY
SCORE _____

New York "Jography" Comes in All Flavors!

Match the type of geography with the area of study it would cover. Score one point for each correct answer. Be sure to cover the bottom of the sheet until you have your answers!

Branch

1. Geography
2. Physiography
3. Mathematical geography
4. Biogeography
5. Oceanography
6. Meteorology
7. Economic geography
8. Anthropography
9. Climatology
10. Political geography

Study

A. Land forms
B. Weather forecasting
C. The physical Earth
D. People and geography
E. Plants, animals
F. Parallels, meridians
G. Waves, tides, currents
H. Industry location
I. Government boundaries
J. Weather

Oooh! I'm taking an ice cream break!

MY ____
SCORE

ANSWERS: 1-C; 2-A; 3-F; 4-E; 5-G; 6-B; 7-H; 8-D; 9-J; 10-I

New York
Our State from A-To-Z!

This should give you a good overview of your state. Take your map and see if you can find a mountain, river, or place for each letter of the alphabet listed here. Score one point for each. (Score two points if you find a Q, U, X, Y, Z!)

A_____

B_____

C_____

D_____

E_____

F_____

G_____

H_____

I_____

J_____

K_____

L_____

M_____

N_____

O_____

P_____

QUICK, YOU'RE DOING GREAT!_____

R_____

S_____

T_____

U CAN DO IT!_____

V_____

W_____

X_____

Y_____

Z_____

MY SCORE ____

New York
A-Maze-ing Capital!

___ ___ ___ ___ ___ ___ ___ is the capital city of New York. Can you find your way through the maze to the capitol building? Score ten points when you arrive!

Are we there yet?

MY ___
SCORE

ANSWERS: Albany

New York
The Great Escape!

Hop on your bike and take a tour of these New York landmarks and attractions. Score a point for each one you can match correctly.

Yikes! Bike Tour

1. The National Baseball Hall of Fame and Museum

2. Times Square

3. American Falls and Bridal Veil Falls

4. International Museum of Photography

5. Boldt Castle

6. Sagamore Hill National Historic Site

7. Genesee Country Village

8. Crailo State Historic Site

9. Statue of Liberty National Monument

10. Children's Museum

A. Manhattan

B. Rochester

C. Utica

D. Liberty Island, New York City

E. Near Oyster Bay, Long Island

F. Cooperstown

G. Rensselaer

H. Niagara Falls

I. Mumford

J. Heart Island

I escaped!

MY SCORE

Over the River and Through the Woods!

See if you can figure out which New York river, lake, mountains, or forest we're looking for—and score a point for each one you figure out!

Keep an Eye to the Sky!

1. Catskill Mountains

2. The Finger Lakes

3. The Palisades

4. The Adirondacks

5. Lake Champlain

6. Niagara River

7. Catskill Park and Forest Preserve

8. Fingers Lake National Forest

9. Lake Chautauqua

10. Genesee River

A. Majestic cliffs at the southern end of the Hudson

B. River at New York's western tip

C. Lake in southwestern New York

D. Mountains west of the Hudson River

E. Forest between Seneca and Cayuga Lakes

F. River in western New York

G. Mountains that cover most of northeastern New York

H. Eleven lakes in north central New York

I. Part of the Catskill Mountains in southeastern New York

J. Lake on the New York and Vermont border

MY SCORE

ANSWERS: 1-D; 2-H; 3-A; 4-G; 5-J; 6-B; 7-I; 8-E; 9-C; 10-F

New York
State Borders

New York is surrounded by other states, mountains, and bodies of water. Can you name New York's borders? Score one point for each border you match.

North to South and East to West!

1. Quebec, Canada
2. Niagara River
3. Long Island Sound
4. Vermont
5. Atlantic Ocean
6. St. Lawrence River
7. New Jersey
8. Lake Erie
9. Connecticut
10. Massachusetts
11. Lake Ontario
12. Ontario, Canada
13. Delaware River
14. Pennsylvania

A. The Green Mountain State to the east
B. Neighbor to the east, home to Boston
C. River separates Ontario, Canada, and New York
D. Eastern neighbor overlooks Long Island Sound
E. Canadian province to the northeast, home to Montreal
F. A big salty sea south and to the east of New York
G. Canadian neighbor, home to Toronto
H. A Great Lake bearing the name of a Canadian province
I. The Garden State, New York's southeastern neighbor
J. Buffalo sits at this lake's eastern edge
K. The Keystone State to the south
L. River at New York's western tip
M. Borders New York's Long Island
N. River to the south, shares Pennsylvania's border

MY SCORE _____

ANSWERS: 1-E; 2-L; 3-M; 4-A; 5-F; 6-C; 7-I; 8-J; 9-D; 10-B; 11-H; 12-G; 13-N; 14-K

Heeey! Wait for me!

See you around!

A Few of My Favorite Things and Places

I'll bet they are yours too! But where in the world are they?!
Score one point for each riddle you solve.

Fun! Fun! Fun! Fun!

1. I am a large and prospering city in far-western New York.
    I bear the name of a large, wooly, Plains animal.
    What am I? _ _ _ _ _ _ _

2. I have five distinct boroughs, each with its own character.
    I am known as "The Big Apple."
    What am I? _ _ _   _ _ _ _   _ _ _ _

3. I am on the Genesee River near its mouth on Lake Ontario.
    I am home to the International Museum of Photography.
    What am I? _ _ _ _ _ _ _ _ _

4. I am a favorite vacation, tourist, and honeymoon destination.
    I am where 500,000 gallons (1.9 million liters) of water go over the
    cliffs every second.
    What am I? _ _ _ _ _ _ _ _   _ _ _ _ _

5. I stretch out into the Atlantic Ocean for 120 miles (193 kilometers).
    I am home to the Hamptons.
    What am I? _ _ _ _   _ _ _ _ _ _

ANSWERS: 1-Buffalo; 2-New York City; 3-Rochester;
4-Niagara Falls; 5-Long Island

MY SCORE _____

New York Football Fever!

If someone gave you season tickets to a game or activity of the schools below—would you know where to find them? Score a point for each school and town you match.

Rah! Rah!! Rah!!!

1. Columbia University

2. U.S. Military Academy

3. Skidmore College

4. Cornell University

5. Vassar College

6. Colgate University

7. Rochester University

8. Syracuse University

9. Bard College

10. State University of New York at Albany

A. Ithaca

B. Hamilton

C. Annondale-on-Hudson

D. New York City

E. Rochester

F. West Point

G. Albany

H. Syracuse

I. Poughkeepsie

J. Saratoga Springs

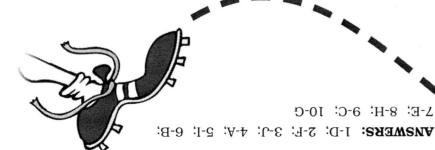

ANSWERS: 1-D; 2-F; 3-J; 4-A; 5-I; 6-B; 7-E; 8-H; 9-C; 10-G

New York
Road Rally!

This is like a scavenger hunt by car! Here are the places on your list. Score one point for each name you complete.

RRRROAD RRRRALLY!

1. A craftsman who makes barrels: C __ __ __ __ __stown

2. This flows from a faucet or fountain: __ __ __ __ __ town

3. It's the color everything turns in the Spring: __ __ __ __ __ __ wood

4. A key unlatches this mechanical part of a door: __ __ __ __ port

5. The first president, Mr. Washington: __ __ __ __ __ __ __ town

6. Put this in the fireplace to make a cozy fire: __ __ __ __ stock

7. The 42nd president of the U.S.: __ __ __ __ __ __ __

8. When blind-folded, you're not to do this: __ __ __ __ skill

9. Don't get this grit in your eyes at the beach: __ __ __ __ usky

10. Ink flows from this writing instrument: __ __ __ nellville

ANSWERS: 1-Cooperstown; 2-Watertown; 3-Greenwood; 4-Lockport; 5-Georgetown; 6-Woodstock; 7-Clinton; 8-Peekskill; 9-Sandusky; 10-Pennellville

MY SCORE ____

New York
Stand Up and Be County-ed!

Score a point for each city you correctly match with its county.

I'm County-ing on You

1. Malone   A. Jefferson

2. Watertown   B. Onondaga

3. Lake Pleasant   C. Franklin

4. Lockport   D. Chautauqua

5. Syracuse   E. Niagara

6. Fonda   F. Steuben

7. Mayville   G. Hamilton

8. Bath   H. Ulster

9. Kingston   I. Suffolk

10. Riverhead   J. Montgomery

ANSWERS: 1-C; 2-A; 3-G; 4-E; 5-B; 6-J; 7-D; 8-F; 9-H; 10-I

Gatorade! Gatorade!

MY SCORE _____

New York
Two-Name Places

How many of these two-name places can you figure out? Score a point for each one you match correctly.

Two for the Price of One!

1. Clifton
2. Rockville
3. Sidney
4. Glen
5. Little

A. Cove
B. Centre
C. Falls
D. Center
E. Springs

Help Glen find his way through the maze to connect with Cove to make up the city of _ _ _ _   _ _ _ _ !

GLEN COVE

ANSWERS: 1-E; 2-B; 3-D; 4-A; 5-C

MY SCORE

New York Instant "Fax!"

There are always a few simple facts about our state we are sure we know. See if that's true! Score one point for each correct fact.

FACTS "R" US!

Official Name: _____

Is The_____ State/Year:_____

Capital: _____

State Nickname:_____

State Motto: _____

State Bird: _____

State Fish:_____

State Tree: _____

State Flower: _____

Greatest Length:_____

Greatest Width:_____

Lowest Point (Name): _____

Highest Point (Name): _____

Number of Counties: _____

MY SCORE ____

New York
You Have a "Date" with History!

Well, of course you'd rather have a date with that cute kid you're crazy about, but this is geography, remember, so... see how well you score with these dates!

(Sometimes) It Was a Very Good Year!

1. 1775

2. 1948

3. 1883

4. 1664

5. 1993

6. 1524

7. 1825

8. 1952

9. 2000

10. 1989

A. Giovanni Da Verrazano sails into New York Harbor

B. The Brooklyn Bridge opens, linking Manhattan with Brooklyn

C. Ethan Allan and Benedict Arnold capture Fort Ticonderoga

D. The Dutch surrender New Amsterdam to England

E. New York City elects David N. Dinkins as first black mayor

F. Completion of Erie Canal connects Albany and Buffalo

G. United Nations Headquarters is completed in New York City

H. The first state university in New York is established

I. Rudolph Giuliani is elected mayor of New York City

J. Hillary Rodham Clinton wins New York Senate seat as nation's first First Lady to run for public office

Isn't it your nap time?

Yeah! Thanks for reminding me.

ANSWERS: 1-C; 2-H; 3-B; 4-D; 5-I; 6-A; 7-F; 8-G; 9-J; 10-E

MY _____
SCORE

New York Festivals!

Jog on down to some of our state's fun festivals and other activities. Score a point for each one you match correctly. Have a great time!

Eat, Drink, and Be Merry!

1. Westminster Kennel Club Dog Show
2. Hudson River White Water Derby
3. Festival of Lilacs
4. Annual Snowbird Soaring Regatta
5. Central New York Scottish Games
6. Festival of Lights
7. Salmon Festival
8. Friendship Festival
9. Schoharie Country Maple Festival
10. Adirondack Hot Air Balloon Festival

A. North Creek
B. Glen Falls
C. Rochester
D. Pulaski
E. Jefferson
F. New York City
G. Liverpool
H. Buffalo
I. Niagara Falls
J. Elmira

ANSWERS: 1-F; 2-A; 3-C; 4-J; 5-G; 6-I; 7-D; 8-H; 9-E; 10-B

It's party time!

MY SCORE ____

Be a Good Sport!

Be a good sport! Score one point each by matching the activity with the most logical place to pursue it!

The Joy of Victory (or the Agony of DA FEET!)

1. Shoot for a goal with the Sabres ice hockey team

2. Rock climb and raft down the rolling river

3. Fly high at the Olympic ski jumps

4. Free-throw with the Knicks and Liberty basketball teams

5. Set sail in the Empire State Regatta

6. Root for the Mets baseball team

7. Watch the Belmont Stakes Horse Race

8. See the Jets and Giants play football

9. Boat, fish, and parasail on the eleven lakes

10. Cheer on the Yankees baseball team

A. Queens, New York City

B. Buffalo

C. Lake Placid

D. Albany

E. Yankee Stadium

F. Long Island

G. The Finger Lakes

H. Madison Square Garden, New York City

I. Hudson River

J. Meadowlands, New Jersey

ANSWERS: 1-B; 2-I; 3-C; 4-H; 5-D; 6-A; 7-F; 8-J; 9-G; 10-E

MY SCORE ____

New York
The Local
Weatherperson–You!

Score one point each if you can fill in the words about our weather. (Do you get a point "weather or not" your answer is correct? NO!)

1. Buffalo, Rochester, and Syracuse get more __ __ __ __ in the Winter than any other big cities in the United States.

2. In much of New York, __ __ __ __ __ __ skies are more common than sunny skies because of the Great Lake's effect.

3. The record __ __ __ __ temperature of 108°F (42°C) was at Troy in 1926.

4. In July, temperatures are __ __ __ __ __ __ on Long Island than in the Adirondacks.

5. In Binghampton, the __ __ __ is totally clear for about sixty-eight days a year.

6. Heavy __ __ __ __ __ in the mountains provide great opportunities to go sledding and skiing.

7. The record low temperature of -52°F (-47°C) was at Old Forge in __ __ __ __.

8. The average July __ __ __ __ __ __ __ __ __ __ __ in New York is 69°F (21°C).

9. In January, temperatures are __ __ __ __ __ __ in the Adirondacks and upstate New York than downstate New York.

10. The average annual precipitation in New York is __ __ inches (__ __ centimeters).

MY SCORE ____

New York
Product Lines!

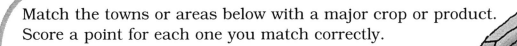

Match the towns or areas below with a major crop or product.
Score a point for each one you match correctly.

1. Books and magazines

2. Medical and surgical equipment

3. Dairy farming

4. Cameras and film

5. Garments (Clothing)

6. Poultry, nursery, and greenhouse items

7. Grapes

8. Shellfish

9. Garnet

10. Apples

A. Lewis County

B. Chinatown, Brooklyn's Sunset Park, and Flushing, Queens

C. New York City

D. Suffolk County, Long Island

E. Long Island Sound

F. Rochester

G. Buffalo

H. North Creek, Warren County

I. Along Lake Ontario and the Hudson River

J. Chautauqua County

MY SCORE ___

New York
Parks and Such

New York has a lot of state parks and such!
Score a point for each one you match correctly.

Where the Wild Things Are!

1. Allegany State Park

2. Bear Mountain State Park

3. Castle Clinton National Monument

4. New York State Museum

5. Museum of Glass

6. Frederic Remington Art Museum

7. Letchworth State Park

8. Watkins Glen State Park

9. Museum of Science

10. Central Park

A. State park in southwestern New York

B. Corning

C. At the southern end of Seneca Lake

D. State park in southeastern New York, near West Point

E. Manhattan

F. Albany

G. Ogdensburg

H. New York City

I. On the Genesee River in western New York

J. Buffalo

ANSWERS: 1-A; 2-D; 3-H; 4-F; 5-B; 6-G; 7-I; 8-C; 9-J; 10-E

MY SCORE

Fifty Nifty States!

Can you match them all? Write each state's two
letter abbreviation in the correct place on the map.
See how many you can get right and add 'em up!

Alabama–AL
Alaska–AK
Arizona–AZ
Arkansas–AR
California–CA
Colorado–CO
Connecticut–CT
Delaware–DE
Florida–FL
Georgia–GA
Hawaii–HI
Idaho–ID
Illinois–IL
Indiana–IN
Iowa–IA
Kansas–KS
Kentucky–KY
Louisiana–LA

Maine–ME
Maryland–MD
Massachusetts–MA
Michigan–MI
Minnesota–MN
Mississippi–MS
Missouri–MO
Montana–MT
Nebraska–NE
Nevada–NV
New Hampshire–NH
New Jersey–NJ
New Mexico–NM
New York–NY
North Carolina–NC
North Dakota–ND
Ohio–OH
Oklahoma–OK

Oregon–OR
Pennsylvania–PA
Rhode Island–RI
South Carolina–SC
South Dakota–SD
Tennessee–TN
Texas–TX
Utah–UT
Vermont–VT
Virginia–VA
Washington–WA
West Virginia–WV
Wisconsin–WI
Wyoming–WY

MY _____
SCORE

New York Scavenger Hunt

Have you ever been on a real-life scavenger hunt? Well, here we go! Score two points for each item you find!

Find and Go Seek!

1. Find a newspaper, magazine, or Internet article about an endangered species from our state. List three endangered species.
   (1) _____
   (2) _____
   (3) _____

2. Find a picture of the state bird. List the bird's colors and any special characteristics.
   Colors: _____
   Special characteristics:_____
   _____

3. What is the governor's name? _____

4. Find a newspaper, magazine, or Internet article about a current event. List the date and main idea(s).
   Date:_____
   Main idea: _____
   _____

5. Listen to a local weather forecast on television or the radio and write down what tomorrow's weather will be. _____
   _____
   _____

These guys are too much!

Heey! Wait for me!

La-La-La La-La...

MY SCORE ____

Manimals

Score one point for each person or animal you match with the place you might find them!

1. Franklin D. Roosevelt, 32nd U.S. President
2. Black bears and snowshoe hares
3. Sojourner Truth, social reformer
4. Beavers, river otters, and muskrats
5. Walt Whitman, author
6. Whales, dolphins, and seals
7. Geraldine Ferraro, lawyer and politician
8. "Cats"
9. John D. Rockefeller, industrialist and philanthropist
10. Dairy cows

A. Hyde Park

B. Richford

C. Newburgh

D. Broadway

E. Near Kingston

F. Farms in upstate New York

G. Rivers and streams throughout New York

H. Long Island Sound and the Atlantic Ocean

I. Adirondack Mountains

J. West Hills, Long Island

ANSWERS: 1-A; 2-I; 3-E; 4-G; 5-J; 6-H; 7-C; 8-D; 9-B; 10-F

Have you seen that other guy?

As a matter of fact, no!

MY SCORE

Keep on jogging and see if you can score two points for each correct answer!

Jog On Down, Jog On Down the Road

1. The geographic center of New York is...
   - A) Albany
   - B) Madison
   - C) Redford

2. Full of trendy art galleries and cafés, ____ has many writers, artists, and musicians.
   - A) Sandwich Village
   - B) Conewango Amish Village
   - C) Greenwich Village

3. Coney Island, a popular amusement park and resort, is at the south end of...
   - A) Brooklyn
   - B) Dayton
   - C) Yonkers

4. Just north of Central Park in New York City is a center of black culture and business enterprises called...
   - A) Wayland
   - B) Harlem
   - C) Pulaski

5. In the 1800s, beautiful scenery in the ____River Valley inspired many artists to paint its landscapes.
   - A) Hudson
   - B) Neversink
   - C) Wallkill

6. The first women's rights convention was held in ____ in 1848.
   - A) Valley Stream
   - B) Sag Harbor
   - C) Seneca Falls

7. ____ overlooks the point were Lake Ontario meets the Niagara River.
   - A) Fort Norton
   - B) Fort Niagara
   - C) Fort Minerva

8. In far western New York, acres of ____ line Lake Erie.
   - A) cactus
   - B) grapevines
   - C) barbed wire

9. The ____ opened in 1825 stretching across the state from Albany on the Hudson to Buffalo on Lake Erie.
   - A) Flannel Canal
   - B) Ear Canal
   - C) Erie Canal

10. New York's first ____, the Mohawk and Hudson, opened in 1831 following the Mohawk River from Albany to Schenectady.
    - A) railroad
    - B) space station
    - C) wagon trail

Just do it!

ANSWERS: 1-B; 2-C; 3-A; 4-B; 5-A; 6-C; 7-B; 8-B; 9-C; 10-A

MY SCORE ____

New York
Jog On Down! II

Keep on jogging and see if you can score two points for each correct answer!

Jog On Down, Jog On Down the Road

1. The Onondaga Nation's reservation is near ____.
   ○ A) Syracuse
   ○ B) Otisco
   ○ C) Virgil

2. Washington Irving's "Rip Van Winkle" took his twenty-year nap in a ravine high in the ____ Mountains.
   ○ A) Rocky
   ○ B) Catskill
   ○ C) Ozark

3. Playing in Carnegie Hall in ____ is the pinnacle of a musician's career.
   ○ A) Manhattan
   ○ B) Holland
   ○ C) Sydney Center

4. ____ came to be called the Island of Tears because so many immigrants were turned away.
   ○ A) Long Island
   ○ B) Ellis Island
   ○ C) Fishers Island

5. Manhattan, Brooklyn, Queens, the Bronx, and Staten Island are New York City's five...
   ○ A) counties
   ○ B) parishes
   ○ C) boroughs

6. The Genesee River is home to the 600-foot (183-meter)...
   ○ A) Genesee River Gorge
   ○ B) Tupper Lake Gorge
   ○ C) Raquette River Gorge

7. The New York State Barge Canal System is one of the ____ inland waterways in the U.S.
   ○ A) shortest
   ○ B) deepest
   ○ C) longest

8. The Thousand Islands region is located along the ____, shared by Ontario, Canada and New York.
   ○ A) Hoosic River
   ○ B) St. Lawrence River
   ○ C) Salmon River

9. Seneca, Cayuga, Placid, Saranac, and Tupper are among New York's largest...
   ○ A) lakes
   ○ B) creeks
   ○ C) reservoirs

10. More snow falls in the ____ southwest of the Adirondacks, than anywhere else east of the Rocky Mountains.
    ○ A) Bug Hill Plateau
    ○ B) Rug Hill Plateau
    ○ C) Tug Hill Plateau

ANSWERS: 1-A; 2-B; 3-A; 4-B; 5-C; 6-A; 7-C; 8-B; 9-A; 10-C

MY SCORE ____

New York
Jogging Through the State

Let's see how many cool places you've visited. Circle the capital city and all the cities you've visited. Then, label all the really fun spots—like amusement parks, museums, and state parks—you've been to or that you think others would enjoy. Score one point for each place you locate.

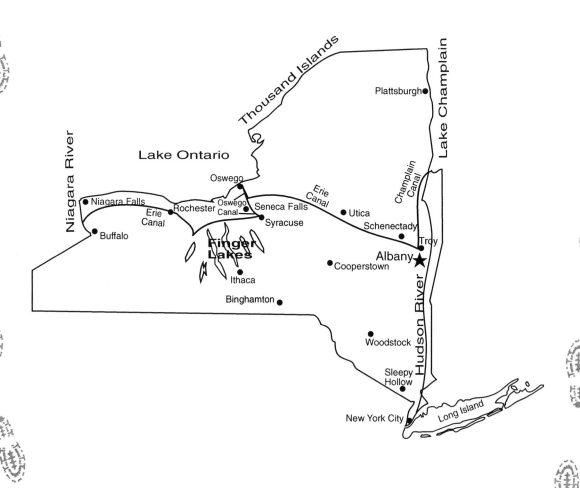

MY SCORE

OK, Jogger, How Did You Score?

SOONER OR LATER ...
you're going to have to find out:

If you scored only a few points—you may not be able to find your way home and back! Try and improve your score—it will be easier the second time.

If you scored a few more—well, maybe you really live in Timbuctu? Timbucktoo? Timbuctwo? Try Again!

If you scored lots of points—this book was meant just for you. Don't take those shoes off! Jog, jog again 'til you can improve your score! I know you can do it!!!

Final Score _____

Make Up Your Own Questions

Here's a place for you to write your own "Jography" questions about places and things in your own hometown.

Quiz your friends! Your parents!! Your teacher!!!

1. _____

2. _____

3. _____

4. _____

5. _____

6. _____

7. _____

8. _____

9. _____

10. _____

I think I'll go write a book!